Questions and Answers About
POLAR
ANIMALS

MICHAEL CHINERY
ILLUSTRATED BY JOHN BUTLER
AND BRIAN MCINTYRE

Kingfisher Books

NEW YORK

KINGFISHER
Larousse Kingfisher Chambers Inc.
95 Madison Avenue
New York, New York 10016

First American edition 1994
10 9 8 7 6 5 4 3 2 1 (HC)
10 9 8 7 6 5 4 3 (PB)

Library of Congress Cataloging-in-Publication Data
Chinery, Michael.
   Questions and answers about polar animals / by
Michael Chinery; illustrated by John Butler and Brian
McIntyre. – 1st American ed.
      p. cm.
   Includes index.
   Zoology – Polar regions – Miscellanea – Juvenile
literature. [1. Zoology – Polar regions.] I. Butler, John, ill.
II. McIntyre, Brian, ill. III. Title. IV. Title: Polar animals.
QL104.C48 1994
591.909'1 – dc20 93-29426 CIP AC

ISBN 1-85697-980-6 (HC)
ISBN 1-85697-964-4 (PB)

Series editor: Mike Halson
Series designer: Terry Woodley
Designer: Dave West Children's Books
Illustrators: John Butler (pp. 1–8, 12–13, 20–22, 24–27,
30–31, 34, 36–38); Brian McIntyre (pp. 9–11, 14–19, 23,
28–29, 32–33, 35)
Cover illustrations: John Butler

Printed in Hong Kong

CONTENTS

What is life like in the polar lands?

The polar lands surround the Earth's north and south poles. The Arctic is the region around the North Pole and the Antarctic surrounds the South Pole. Both regions are very cold, with temperatures below freezing for most of the year. Even in the summer they do not rise above 50°F. The sea freezes in the winter to form pack ice. Polar animals have thick coats to keep them warm. Those living in the icy water also have a thick layer of fat, called blubber, under the skin.

This picture shows a scene from the Arctic. This region consists mainly of a treeless land, called the tundra, surrounding the Arctic Ocean. It has many more animals than the Antarctic because the tundra snow melts in the summer and animals can feed on the plants growing there.

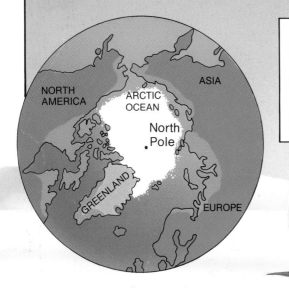

NORTH AMERICA

ASIA

ARCTIC OCEAN

North Pole

GREENLAND

EUROPE

KEY TO POLAR MAPS

Sea covered with ice for all or much of the year

Land permanently covered with ice and snow

Tundra

DO YOU KNOW

Polar mammals usually have smaller ears and shorter snouts than similar animals that live in warmer climates. This is all to do with their need to keep as warm as they can in bitterly cold temperatures. Heat is easily lost from long ears and noses, so it is best to have short ones in cold climates.

THE ANTARCTIC

This is an icy land surrounded by cold seas. Even in the summer most of the land is covered with ice. Almost all the Antarctic animals live in the sea, where there are lots of fish and other creatures for them to feed on.

SOUTHERN OCEAN

SOUTH AMERICA

• South Pole

SOUTHERN OCEAN

What do polar bears eat?

Polar bears live around the coasts of the Arctic Ocean. They sometimes swim far out to sea, but usually stay close to the pack ice. That is where they find the seals that make up most of their diet. They also catch fish, and when they come ashore in the summer they even eat berries. Polar bears are very strong and dangerous animals. In Canada they sometimes raid towns and villages and break into buildings to find food.

 SURVIVAL WATCH

Polar bears are quite rare and most northern countries have laws to protect them, although hunters still kill a few each year. Bears that raided towns used to be shot, but they are now caught and flown back to the wild.

The bear's broad feet are like snowshoes. Hairy soles help them to grip the slippery ice and snow.

Polar bears are great swimmers. They paddle with their front legs and use their hind legs as rudders.

Polar bear cubs are born under the snow in midwinter. They weigh less than 2 pounds at birth.

The polar bear has huge teeth for tearing its prey apart. Its tongue is a strange violet color.

 **DO YOU KNOW**

A bear often waits by a seal's breathing hole and kills the seal as it comes up for air. This is easier than chasing seals over the ice. The bear eats the seal's skin and fat and the internal organs, but not the meat.

Oily fur and a thick layer of fat under the skin keep the polar bear warm even in the coldest weather.

 POLAR BEAR FACTS

● Adults weigh 650–1,100 pounds. They can run at 20 mph and swim at 26 mph.

● Polar bears catch ducks and geese as well as seals and fish.

How do lemmings control their numbers?

Lemmings are the most common mammals on the northern tundra. They are about 6 inches long and look a bit like hamsters. They feed on grasses and other tundra plants, and are themselves eaten by stoats, foxes, and snowy owls. Every few years the number of lemmings increases so much that there is not enough food for them. Millions of them then rush over the tundra in search of new homes and a new source of food.

Lemmings spend the winter in long, winding tunnels which they dig through the snow at ground level. They even have some of their babies there.

Coming up for a bit of fresh air, this lemming must keep its eyes and ears open for stoats and other hungry predators.

? DO YOU KNOW

Many lemmings drown crossing rivers. Some people say that they kill themselves on purpose, but they are just trying to find new homes. The lucky ones are those that stayed behind. They have plenty of food and can start again.

Lemmings find plenty of food in their winter tunnels. The thick blanket of snow above keeps them surprisingly warm.

What sends the snowy owl south?

The snowy owl is up to 2 feet long and is one of the world's hardiest birds. It lives on the tundra all through the year, although it may fly far to the south if food is short. Lemmings are its favorite food, but it also catches rabbits, hares, and ducks. The female lays up to 15 eggs in a hollow on the ground. She does not make a real nest.

DO YOU KNOW

The number of snowy owls varies greatly. They can rear lots of chicks when lemmings are plentiful, so their population goes up. In years when lemmings are scarce, many owls starve and their numbers fall again.

With its large eyes the owl can hunt well either in darkness or in the long daylight hours of the summer.

Dense feathers on the legs and feet help keep the snowy owl warm. The strong talons are used to snatch its prey.

The female owl's speckled feathers help to camouflage her while she sits on the ground guarding her eggs and young.

How do butterflies survive in the Arctic?

There are no butterflies in the Antarctic because there are no flowers for them to feed on, but it is a different story in the Arctic. The tundra is covered with flowers in the summer and many pretty butterflies live there. Before they become fully developed butterflies, the caterpillars and chrysalises are protected against the cold by a special fluid in their bodies. This acts like car antifreeze and stops them freezing solid.

DO YOU KNOW

Polar butterflies are darker than those in warmer areas. Dark colors soak up heat better than pale ones, so the butterflies warm up more quickly by having darker colors.

The Arctic fritillary warms its muscles ready for flight by basking in the weak sunshine with its wings open.

Caterpillars hatching from the eggs of the northern clouded yellow will take two years to grow up in the cold climate.

Where do eider ducks gather food?

Eider ducks are sturdy ducks that normally live on the Arctic coasts. The males are largely black and white, but the females are dull brown. Eider ducks are great divers and feed mainly on shellfish that they collect on the seabed. The common eider pictured here often flies south for the winter and may get as far as the Mediterranean Sea.

EIDER DUCK FACTS

● Several kinds of eider ducks live in the far north.

● The spectacled eider is named for its pale eye patches, which make it look as if it is wearing glasses.

The nest is a hollow lined with seaweed and filled with down from the female's breast. There are up to six eggs.

DO YOU KNOW

The "eiderdowns" that many people put on their beds are so named because they are filled with the soft, downy feathers of the female eider duck. The feathers are also used to stuff pillows.

Eider ducks like company and they often swim in large flocks. They also nest in colonies, usually close to the sea.

Who looks after a penguin egg?

Emperor penguins spend all their lives on and around the Antarctic ice. The female lays a single egg in the middle of the winter in temperatures as low as $-112°F$. The male looks after the egg while the female goes fishing. She may have to walk more than 60 miles to the water and she stays away for about 60 days. But she knows exactly when to go back. She returns with a supply of fish just as the egg is ready to hatch. The poor male is starving and very thin by this time and he waddles off to the sea to feed.

PENGUIN FACTS

● At 4 feet high, emperors are the largest penguins. They breed in huge colonies called rookeries.

● All penguins live in the Southern Hemisphere, but not all live in cold places. Some kinds live in warm seas near the equator.

The male holds the egg between his feet and his belly. The egg would die if it touched the ice.

The growing chicks huddle together for warmth while their parents are both away fishing.

The chicks lose their fluffy coats and get shiny adult feathers when they are about four months old.

DO YOU KNOW

? **DO YOU KNOW**

Penguins cannot fly through the air, but they flap their strong, flipperlike wings in the water just as if they were flying. Emperor penguins dive down more than 160 feet to catch fish.

Penguins have scaly, waterproof feathers and a thick layer of fat underneath to keep them warm.

This young chick is about to move onto its mother's feet and get its first meal of fish from her.

Whose leftovers do Arctic foxes eat?

Arctic foxes roam all over the far north, including some of the icy islands of the Arctic Ocean. Lemmings are their main food, but they will eat almost anything, including ptarmigan and seaweed. Foxes living in the northernmost areas follow polar bears in the winter and feed on the remains of the seals killed by the bears.

The ears are short, as long ones would lose too much body warmth to the air.

The summer coat is usually grayish brown, but the fox grows a thick white coat for the winter months.

Arctic fox cubs are born in an underground den during the summer. There are usually about seven cubs in a litter. Both parents bring them food.

Can a ptarmigan fly?

The ptarmigan spends all its life in the cold, either on the northern tundra or in the mountains. Like many other Arctic animals, it turns white for the winter so that it stays well camouflaged all year round. The ptarmigan spends most of its time on the ground, but it flies perfectly well in a series of glides alternating with a rapid whirring of its wings.

DO YOU KNOW

Short autumn days are what cause the ptarmigan to grow its white winter coat. If the bird is kept in captivity with less than 12 hours of light each day, its coat will turn white—even in the middle of summer.

The ptarmigan's legs and feet are clothed with feathers that help to keep them warm in the snow.

Ptarmigan have many enemies, and often have to take action to avoid being spotted. When they are alarmed they crouch down and use their camouflage to blend in with the ground.

In late spring, the female lays up to ten well-camouflaged eggs in a bare hollow on the ground.

The ptarmigan feeds mainly on leaves and shoots, but it also likes to eat berries in the fall.

How fast can wolves run?

The wolf is the biggest member of the dog family. It hunts over the Arctic tundra in packs. Each pack normally has between eight and 15 animals and is led by the strongest male and his mate. Wolves eat just about any kind of animal, but they usually take the largest they can get. Reindeer are their main prey on the tundra and the pack members work together to catch them. They call to each other with loud howls. Wolves can run for hours at about 25 miles per hour and chase their prey until it is exhausted.

SURVIVAL WATCH

Wolves once lived in countries all over the Northern Hemisphere, but now they live only in really wild areas. Elsewhere they have been wiped out because they were a menace to sheep and other farm animals.

Tundra wolves are usually a yellowish gray color, but sometimes they are white—especially in North America.

The leading female gives birth to about seven cubs in a den among the rocks. The other females help to guard the cubs.

Young wolf cubs spend a lot of time playing. When they are bigger, their parents teach them how to hunt.

Each wolf pack roams an area called a home range. This may cover more than 200 square miles. Some packs move south into the forests for the winter.

 **DO YOU KNOW**

The position of a wolf's tail tells other wolves what mood it is in. A straight tail (1) warns them to keep away. A tail pressed down against the legs (2) means "I give in, don't attack me." A drooping tail (3) means a contented wolf.

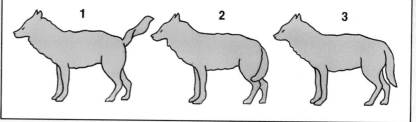

Wolves have large stabbing teeth for killing their prey, as well as sharp-edged cheek teeth for slicing up the meat.

 **WOLF FACTS**

• The wolf is up to 6 feet long and can weigh 150 pounds.

• Wolves can eat 30 pounds of meat in one meal and then not eat again for weeks.

How do snow buntings hide in the tundra?

Snow buntings nest on the stony ground of the tundra. The female's brown feathers help to camouflage her on the nest. The males look like big snowflakes when flocks of them swoop over the tundra in summer.

The snow bunting's stout beak is used mainly for crushing seeds. The bird also eats insects.

Where do bluethroats sing?

The cheerful song of the male bluethroat can be heard all over the tundra of Europe and Asia in the summer. Bluethroats find plenty of insects and small seeds to eat among the dwarf willow bushes.

 DO YOU KNOW

The bluethroat is only $5\frac{1}{2}$ inches long, but when fall comes it flies all the way to Africa or southern Asia. It flies back to the north to nest in the spring. These long journeys are called migrations.

Male bluethroats have a red or white spot on their throat. Females have no blue on them at all.

Which country has the most gyrfalcons?

The gyrfalcon is a powerful bird of prey about 2 feet long. It spends all year on the tundra or on rocky coasts in and around the Arctic. Its favorite prey is the ptarmigan, which it catches in the air or on the ground. Gyrfalcons nest on rocky ledges and often take over the old nests of other large birds. Most gyrfalcons live in Greenland.

SURVIVAL WATCH

Gyrfalcon populations have fallen alarmingly in the last 50 years because the birds have been poisoned by pesticides. This does not actually kill them, but it prevents the falcons from rearing many chicks.

Like all falcons, the gyrfalcon has long, narrow wings and can fly at very high speeds.

Gyrfalcons rear three or four chicks. The chicks can fly when they are about seven weeks old.

Gyrfalcons from Greenland and the far north are almost white, but farther south the birds are mainly dark gray.

What do Adélie penguins do in winter?

The Adélie is one of the commonest of the 17 types of penguin. At about 18 inches high, it is also one of the smallest. Adélies spend the long winter feeding on shrimplike creatures in the freezing seas of Antarctica. They return to the land to rear their chicks in the spring. Each pair uses the same rocky nest site every year. Penguins cannot fly, but they can swim superbly with their flipperlike wings.

 **ADÉLIE FACTS**

● There are usually two eggs in a nest. The male and female take turns to guard them.

● When the chicks are about a month old they leave the nest and join hundreds of others in groups called creches. Their parents regularly take them food.

To travel at speed, Adélies slide along on their bellies. They use their narrow wings and webbed feet to push and steer.

Adélies feed their chicks with partly digested food. The baby penguin takes the food from inside its parent's mouth.

To make the nest, the male Adélie fetches pebbles and drops them at his mate's feet. She sets them out in a small circle.

Chinstrap penguins (left) get their name from the line running below their chin. Macaronies (right) are named for fancily dressed gentlemen known as "macaronies" 200 years ago.

When the male finds his old nest he warns others to keep away by looking up at the sky, waving his wings and calling loudly.

Getting from the water on to the ice is no problem for the Adélie —it can leap more than 6 feet straight up into the air.

As well as being superb underwater swimmers, Adélies are quite at home paddling around on the surface like ducks.

Why do stoats change color in the fall?

The stoat is a small but powerful and fast-running hunter found in the northern regions of Europe and Asia. Birds and voles are its main prey on the northern tundra, but elsewhere it eats a lot of rabbits. In the northernmost areas it grows a white coat, called ermine, in the fall, and is then well camouflaged when the snow comes.

STOAT FACTS

● Males are about a foot long and weigh up to a pound. Females are smaller.

● The tip of the stoat's tail is always black, even in the winter when the rest of the animal's fur is white.

The female stoat may have 12 babies in the spring. She often carries them to new homes in her mouth.

The stoat's white winter coat is called ermine. The white fur is widely used for decorating clothes.

Who are the polar pirates?

Skuas are often called pirates because they chase other seabirds and steal fish from them, although they are perfectly capable of catching fish for themselves. The great skua seen here is also a major predator of gulls and penguins. It is the only seabird that breeds in the far north as well as in the Antarctic. The great skua is a fearless bird and will dive at people and clout them with its wings if they get too near its nest.

Skuas often work in pairs. Here, the first one is sweeping down to knock over an adult penguin. Behind it, another skua is preparing to zoom down and grab the helpless chick. The birds also take penguin eggs in the same way.

The skua's main weapon is its powerful beak, with which it can easily kill a penguin chick.

? DO YOU KNOW

Great skuas once lived only in the Southern Hemisphere, but they have now spread to the north. There are great skua colonies in Iceland, the Shetland Isles, and Scotland.

How do musk oxen survive blizzards?

The musk ox is one of the world's hardiest mammals. It spends all the year on the tundra and, thanks to its long coat, it can survive blizzards with temperatures as low as −40°F. Musk oxen live in small herds. They eat grasses and dwarf willows in the summer, but in the winter they depend mainly on lichens and on fat stored up in their bodies during the summer. The musk ox weighs 900 pounds and is 4 feet high.

Wolves are the musk ox's only natural enemies, but they attack only young or weak animals. A pack of wolves would have no chance against this ring of adult musk oxen.

The long, thick coat gives the musk ox good protection from the cold. Babies have thick coats when they are born.

Broad hooves help the musk ox to walk on soft snow. They are also used for sweeping the snow away from food.

SURVIVAL WATCH

Musk oxen once roamed all over the tundra, but they were easy targets for hunters. Hunting was stopped just in time to save the species from extinction and musk oxen are now quite common again. Most of them live in Canada and Greenland.

INSIDE THE RING

The ring formation keeps the young and weak members of the herd safe from wolves.

The curtain of long thick fur also gives valuable shelter from the wind and snow.

Adult musk oxen

Youngsters safe from harm

The horns are about 2 feet long. They are a very good defense against wolves, but not against the bullets from a hunter's rifle.

How far do Arctic terns travel?

The Arctic tern makes the longest of all animal journeys. At the end of every summer, after breeding in and around the Arctic, it flies away to spend the next few months fishing in the Antarctic Ocean. And then it flies back to the north to breed again. The round trip may be as much as 25,000 miles, but it means that the bird spends almost all its life in daylight.

DO YOU KNOW

A male tern attracts a mate by gliding over the colony with a fish in his beak. He gives it to any female who flies up to meet him, and then the birds may pair up.

The Arctic tern usually flies with its beak facing down. Its flight is rather slow and bouncing.

Terns feed mainly at sea. They hover over the water and then plunge down to snatch fish in their beaks.

Arctic tern chicks are well camouflaged in their nests, built on the Arctic tundra or on stony beaches.

Where do snow geese go for the winter?

Snow geese nest in huge colonies by the tundra pools of North America and Siberia in the summer. They feed mainly on the lush grasses that grow there. The geese fly south in the fall to spend the winter up to 3,000 miles away in Mexico, California, and Japan.

SNOW GOOSE FACTS

- Snow geese weigh up to 13 pounds.

- Some snow geese are white, while others are a bluish gray.

Why does a female dotterel leave her mate?

The dotterel has found a way of producing two broods of chicks during the short Arctic summer. The female leaves the male to rear her chicks and often finds a second mate. Dotterels breed on the tundra of Europe and Asia, and fly to Africa for the winter.

DO YOU KNOW

Dotterels are very tame birds. They are so trusting that they will sometimes allow themselves to be stroked while sitting on their nests.

What is the name of the smallest seal?

The ringed seal, named for its ringlike markings, is the world's smallest seal. It is only about 5 feet long. Most ringed seals stay on or under the Arctic ice all through the year. They feed mainly on shrimps and other small crustaceans.

DO YOU KNOW

Seals swimming under the thick Arctic ice need to come up for air every few minutes. To do this they have to chew breathing holes through the ice with their teeth.

Ringed seals live farther north than any other mammal. There are probably about six million of them in the frozen Arctic waters.

What makes the narwhal unusual?

The narwhal is a small Arctic whale with no teeth except for its long tusk. It feeds mainly on squid, which it grabs with its hardened gums. The tusk is found only in the male narwhal and is up to 9 feet long—half as long as the whale's body.

DO YOU KNOW

Eskimos carve narwhal tusks into good luck charms. But we still don't really know what the narwhals use their tusks for!

Where do northern fur seals breed?

This big seal lives in the northern part of the Pacific Ocean, and only rarely strays into the icy waters of the Arctic Ocean. It feeds mostly on fish and squid. In the summer, the northern fur seals come ashore on a group of islands near Alaska to breed. Each big male, or bull, claims a section of the beach and drives other males away. He mates with as many cows, or females, as he can collect on his piece of the shore.

SURVIVAL WATCH

There were over two million northern fur seals when they were discovered about 200 years ago, but in just 100 years fur hunters killed nearly all of them. Hunting is now carefully controlled and the seals are doing well again.

The male has a thick fur cape. He weighs up to 600 pounds and is very much bigger than the female.

The back flippers can be turned forward. Small nails on these flippers are used for grooming the fur.

What is the name of the largest seal?

Elephant seals are the world's biggest seals. The males, or bulls, are probably the ugliest as well. The seals come ashore on rocky beaches to breed in the spring. The males arrive first and the biggest and strongest ones each take a stretch of the beach for themselves. They are called beachmasters. The females, or cows, arrive a little later and each beachmaster herds as many as he can into his territory. The females are already pregnant from last year, and they have their pups soon after they arrive. They are then ready to mate with their beachmasters.

The male's snout is a bit like an elephant's trunk. It is used to make bellowing roars that can be heard more than a mile away.

When two bull elephant seals want the same stretch of beach, they fight to decide who gets it. The weaker male eventually gives up and slinks away.

Fighting bulls often rip chunks of flesh from each other with their teeth. The wounds heal quickly but leave ugly scars.

The southern elephant seals shown here live in the Southern Ocean. Their relatives, the northern elephant seals, live in the warm waters of Mexico and California.

Despite their size, elephant seals feed on small fish and squid.

ELEPHANT SEAL FACTS

● Bull elephant seals are up to 20 feet long and weigh 4 tons.

● Newborn pups weigh 90 pounds, but when they leave their mothers a month later they weigh 330 pounds!

A beachmaster may round up and defend a "harem" of 100 females, but 20–30 is a more usual number.

The beachmaster weighs up to four times as much as the cow. He mates with every cow in his harem.

Do grizzly bears eat only meat?

Someone once described the grizzly bear as four legs and a bunch of claws. It weighs up to 1,000 pounds and is a very powerful and dangerous animal. Although it belongs to the flesh-eating group of mammals, it eats a lot of vegetable food—especially in the fall when berries and other fruits are plentiful. It will actually eat more or less anything that it finds, including other animals' leftovers.

Grizzly bears are very fond of salmon, which they catch by flipping the fish out of the water with their huge paws.

SURVIVAL WATCH

Grizzly bears once roamed all over the western part of North America, but settlers killed most of them to safeguard their cattle. Grizzlies now live only in the far north and in some mountain areas farther south.

Grizzly bear cubs stay with their mothers for about two years while they learn how to hunt.

Huge paws with sharp claws are the bear's main weapons. They can kill a moose with a single swipe.

When do mountain hares grow new coats?

Mountain hares, also known as Arctic hares, live all over the Arctic tundra as well as on many mountains further south. The hares are grayish brown in the summer, but as the temperature falls in the autumn they grow new white coats ready for the winter. They often live in large groups and sometimes dig shallow burrows for shelter in cold weather.

Mountain hares have shorter ears than other hares, so they do not lose too much heat to the cold air.

Mountain hares also have shorter snouts than other hares—another way of saving body warmth.

 **HARE FACTS**

● The mountain hare is up to 2 feet long. It generally feeds on heather and other dwarf shrubs.

● The mountain hares of Ireland, where there is not much snow, do not go white in winter.

How do walruses stay warm?

The walrus is a cousin of the seals. It is up to 12 feet long and can weigh 3,300 pounds. The tusks are the walrus's front teeth and they are up to 3 feet long. They are used for defense and for getting food. The walrus is rather clumsy on land but, like all seals, it is an excellent swimmer. A thick layer of blubber under its skin keeps the walrus warm in its Arctic home.

Walruses like to sunbathe in large groups on rocky shores and ice floes. They are noisy creatures and roar loudly if disturbed.

 **DO YOU KNOW**

The walrus digs shellfish from the seabed with its tusks. The tusks are not big enough for digging until a walrus is nearly two years old. Until then it feeds on its mother's milk.

The walrus has reddish hair when young, but older animals often become almost bald.

The walrus's sensitive mustache helps it to separate shellfish from stones on the seabed.

 SURVIVAL WATCH

Huge numbers of walruses were killed in the 1800s for their meat, skins, and tusks. They became quite rare, but hunting is now controlled and the walruses are safe.

What do crabeater seals really eat?

Crabeater seals do not actually eat crabs. They feed on tiny animals drifting near the surface of the sea. Specially designed teeth fit together like a sieve to strain the food from the water. Millions of crabeater seals live on and around the Antarctic pack ice.

 **CRABEATER FACTS**

● Crabeater seals are white in summer and silvery gray in winter.

● They live in packs and are probably the commonest seals.

The crabeater does not need strong jaw muscles, so its snout is smaller than that of most seals.

Which seal has an unusual coat?

The leopard seal was named for its spotted coat. It can be up to 12 feet long and is the largest of the Antarctic seals. It lives alone and feeds mainly on fish and squid, but also catches penguins around the pack ice.

The seal's long head contains powerful jaw muscles and some large teeth which can easily slice up a big fish or a penguin.

What is special about reindeer antlers?

Reindeer live in herds all over the tundra region. In the summer they feed on the tundra grasses and lichens, but they usually move south to the shelter of the forests for the winter. Reindeer are the only deer where the females have antlers as well as the males. The males lose their antlers after the fall mating season and grow new ones in the spring, but the females change their antlers in the summer. The North American caribou is related to the reindeer.

REINDEER FACTS

● Reindeer are about 4 feet high at the shoulder. The male is called a stag and the female a hind.

● Like all deer, they eat their fallen antlers. This helps them grow strong new ones.

The reindeer's coat is thick and very warm. It is gray in the winter but it changes to a rich brown color for the summer.

Reindeer find food in winter by shoveling the snow away with their big hooves. The name caribou is a Native American word for "shoveler."

Antlers are made of bone and are covered with skin at first. The male's antlers are larger than those of the female.

Broad hooves act like snowshoes, helping the reindeer to walk over soft snow without sinking too far into it.

Reindeer are good swimmers and often cross large rivers on their annual journeys from the tundra to the forest and back.

? DO YOU KNOW

Most of the reindeer of northern Europe and Asia have been domesticated, or tamed. They provide meat, milk, and leather just as cattle do in other regions. And reindeer sleighs are often the best way of getting around in the snow—just ask Santa Claus!

Why are some polar animals in danger?

Huge amounts of oil and coal have recently been discovered under the frozen soils of the Arctic tundra. There are also deposits of important minerals, including the metals copper and gold. Despite the intense cold and the long periods of darkness, people are moving into these northern lands to get at the minerals. New towns have been built near the mines and oil wells, and the animal life has suffered in many areas.

Even the ice-covered Arctic Ocean is not safe from human activity because oil and other poisonous materials get into the sea and harm the fish and other animals living there.

SAVING ANTARCTICA

Antarctica probably has a lot of valuable minerals and oil under its ice, but the world's countries recently agreed not to damage this beautiful region by mining or drilling for oil. Many scientists live and work in Antarctica, studying the Earth's climate and atmosphere, but they do not harm the continent or its wildlife.

Oil pipelines stretching across the Arctic tundra can upset the balance of nature by warming the land and by interfering with animal migration.

Useful words

Bird of prey   Any bird belonging to the hawk and eagle group, with strong claws and a hooked beak. These birds feed on a wide range of other animals.

Blizzard   A severe snowstorm with strong winds.

Blubber   The thick layer of fat found under the skin of many polar animals. It helps to keep them warm.

Brood   The name given to a group of young animals, especially birds or insects, that hatch from one batch of eggs.

Camouflage   The way in which animals avoid the attention of their enemies by resembling their surroundings or blending in with them. The animals are then not easy to see.

Chrysalis   The resting stage in the life history of a butterfly or moth, as it changes from a crawling caterpillar into the flying adult insect.

Climate   The general weather conditions of an area, due largely to the area's position on the Earth's surface.

Crustacean   Any member of the lobster and crab group of animals—hard-shelled creatures with lots of legs.

Domesticated   Not wild. Domesticated animals have been tamed by people for various purposes.

Extinction   The dying out of any kind of plant or animal. An extinct creature is one that no longer lives anywhere on Earth.

Hemisphere   One half of the world. The Northern Hemisphere is the northern half and the Southern Hemisphere is the southern half. They are separated by an imaginary line called the equator.

Lichen   A very hardy type of plant that covers much of the tundra. Some lichens can grow on solid rock. Lichens have no flowers.

Litter   The name given to a group of baby mammals that are all born at the same time.

Mammal   Any member of the large group of animals that feed their babies with milk from the mother's body. Most mammals have hair or fur, and this is especially thick in many polar mammals.

Migration   The regular movement of animals from one area to another at certain seasons. Many polar animals migrate to warmer lands for the winter.

Pesticide   A poison used to kill pests.

Predator   Any animal that hunts or traps other animals for food.

Prey   Any animal that is caught and eaten by a predator.

Tundra   The cold, treeless area of land surrounding the Arctic Ocean. It is frozen in the winter, but the ice melts in the summer and the tundra is then covered with colorful plants.

Tusk   A long and usually pointed tooth, used for fighting and also for digging up food.

Index